For Sue, Joni, and Wendy —K. C.

Tutu: Mom

From: The Sugar Pun Fairy —M. I.

Text copyright © 2015 by Kristyn Crow
Illustrations copyright © 2015 by Molly Idle

First published in the United States of America in September 2015
by Bloomsbury Children's Books
www.bloomsbury.com

Bloomsbury is a registered trademark of Bloomsbury Publishing Plc

For information about permission to reproduce selections from this book, write to
Permissions, Bloomsbury Children's Books, 1385 Broadway, New York, New York 10018
Bloomsbury books may be purchased for business or promotional use. For information on bulk purchases please contact
Macmillan Corporate and Premium Sales Department at specialmarkets@macmillan.com

Library of Congress Cataloging-in-Publication Data
available upon request
ISBN 978-1-61963-640-8 (hardcover)
ISBN 978-1-61963-810-5 (e-book) • ISBN 978-1-61963-811-2 (e-PDF)

Art created with Prismacolor pencils on vellum-finish Bristol
Typeset in Oldbook ITC Std
Book design by Regina Flath and Yelena Safronova

Printed in China by Leo Paper Products, Heshan, Guangdong
1 3 5 7 9 10 8 6 4 2

Zombelina
Dances The Nutcracker

Kristyn Crow

illustrated by
Molly Idle

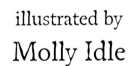

BLOOMSBURY
NEW YORK   LONDON   NEW DELHI   SYDNEY

It's me, Zombelina, at tryouts today . . .
in the old opera house with my CORPSE de ballet.
I'm here for *The Nutcracker*. It's my audition.
And I know I'm going to be STIFF competition!

I hope Grandpa Phantom will give me some space.

For ninety-nine years he's been haunting this place.

My grandpa's a trickster, and I've got to focus.

I can't be distracted by his hocus-pocus.

They call me onstage right beside Lizzie Snow,
who's one of the very best dancers I know.
She's trying for Clara . . . the role of *my* dreams!
I'm nervous enough I could burst at the seams!

I pas de bourrée and jeté in midair.

But Lizzie piqués with her own savoir faire!
The judges are silent. She's got their attention . . .

. . . till I make them gasp at my wicked extension.

We wait for the cast list. I'm scared half to death!
Lizzie looks pale, and she's holding her breath.

What's this?

Me?

I get to be Clara! The role is now mine!

I won't ROT AWAY in the dull chorus line!

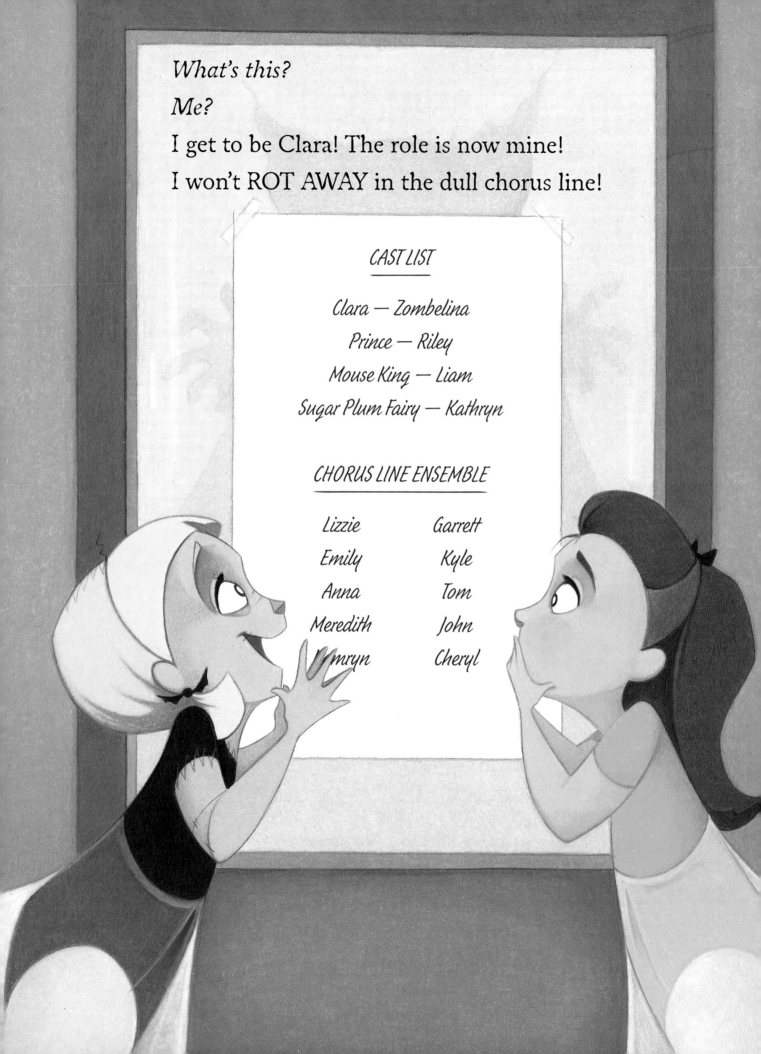

CAST LIST
_____

Clara — Zombelina

Prince — Riley

Mouse King — Liam

Sugar Plum Fairy — Kathryn

CHORUS LINE ENSEMBLE
_____

Lizzie	Garrett
Emily	Kyle
Anna	Tom
Meredith	John
Kamryn	Cheryl

I feel bad for Lizzie. Believe me, I do.
She says, "Zombelina, I'm happy for you."

But then she gets tearful. I hug her and say,
"Oh, Lizzie, you'll have your big moment someday."

We wave at rehearsals.
She says I'm "*Superbe!*"

And during our breaks we share snacks on the curb.

Performance day comes, and my poor tummy churns.
I dress up as Clara and practice my turns.

The crowd is enormous! Not one empty seat!
And then . . . it's dead silent. My heart doesn't beat.
The theater gets dark. There's a thrill in the air.
The notes of Tchaikovsky ring out everywhere.

The sets and the costumes
are such a delight!

The Christmas tree glows
with a magical light.

I wave the nutcracker
and hold him up high—

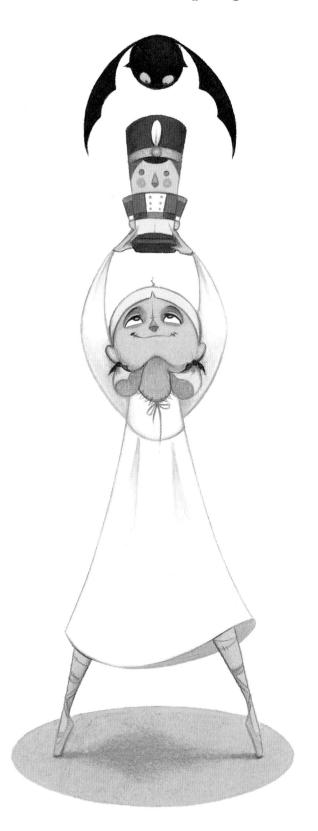

I relevé . . .

sauté . . .

and make Clara fly!

But next on the stage
is the dreaded Mouse King.
He battles the prince,
and their sharp sabers swing!

When it's the right moment I take off my shoe
to throw it at him (just as Clara must do),

but oh, what a mess . . .
as you'd probably guess—
my foot ends up sailing along with it too!

I get it together, then dance to the sleigh—
to leave with the prince for a land far away.

But wait—what's that shadow up high on the planks?
Why it's Grandpa Phantom! He's pulling his pranks!

"HEE HEE HEE HEE HEE!"

If I don't stop Grandpa, he'll conjure more tricks!
This is a disaster that I'd better fix!
I'm in the next scene . . .
How can I save the show?
And then I remember my friend
Lizzie Snow.

I have an idea. "It's *your* moment now! Take *my* place as Clara!"
And Lizzie asks, "How?"

"I don't know the steps," she says. "What should I do?"
I stare in a trance, just to think it all through.

"At times everyone needs a leg up," I say.
"My limbs have a life of their own, anyway.
So tuck in your legs, and let mine dance the show.
With Clara's long nightgown, they won't even know!"

Lizzie looks squeamish but nods an okay.
"I've heard 'break a leg,' but . . . never this way."

I get to the light box and reset the fuse—
make Grandpa an offer that he can't refuse:
to play me in hangman! (That's his favorite game.)
The show must go on, though it isn't the same.

From backstage I soon hear the orchestra start.
I watch Lizzie dance, and it warms my cool heart.

At curtain call, finally, I'm back on my feet.
And Lizzie's big smile makes
the whole night complete.

A spine-tingling finish despite all my fears!
The cast lifts me up, and the audience cheers!

A standing ovation! A real thrilling sight!
Merry Christmas to all, and to all a good *fright*!